Site Dreams

(MOUNT ROYAL ENGLISH DEPARTMENT)

Site Dreams

S.M. Longbottom

Thistledown Press Ltd.

© 1993, S.M. Longbottom
Second printing, 1997
This book was first published in the New Leaf Editions series.

Canadian Cataloguing in Publication Data
Longbottom, S. M. (Suzanne M.), 1966–

Site dreams

(New leaf editions)
ISBN 1–895449–11–1

I. Title. II. Series.

PS8573.O54S5 1993   C813'.54   C93–098143–X
PR9199.3.L6585 1993

Book design by A.M. Forrie
Typeset in 11 pt. Goudy by Thistledown Press Ltd.

Printed and bound in Canada by
Veilleux Impression à Demande Inc.
Boucherville, Quebec

Cover painting
Man Alone (1963) by Ivan Eyre
oil on canvas
81.3cm X 66.0 cm.
Transparency courtesy of the artist
Collection of the Edmonton Art Gallery

Thistledown Press Ltd.
633 Main Street
Saskatoon, Saskatchewan
S7H 0J8

Thistledown Press acknowledges the support received for its publishing program from the Saskatchewan Arts Board and the Canada Council Block Grant program.

Site Dreams

1

"I am Paul, seer of the future, dreamer of the past, named after a poet," Paul liked to say to himself when the morning sun could be seen over the tops of half-demolished oil derricks and grain silos. "I am a garbage picker in the Landfill called Saskatchewan." A gust of wind came up, drying his lips, his eyes. "Today, I will touch garbage of the dead, smell the fresher trash from the East, rub my shoulders into the oily dirt, taste the sour air of mice crushed and rotting in combines I help to tear apart. I am Paul." Paul knew why he chanted this; every day was the same in the heap. He longed for an adventure, a quirk in the routine of wake, eat, pick, nap, eat, pick and sleep.

Outside his tractor-tire and sheetmetal shelter, the wind picked up a strip of plastic and blew it across a naked patch of ground, scuttling it here and there between the old cars, around the dusty, oil-soaked circle of the cooking flame where the tribe would soon come to eat the first meal. Paul shivered as the wind hummed in an empty combine hopper.

The other shelters were on the far side of the cooking flame. Alone, away from the rest, Paul could sit and think. It was here his visions came. The train was due back any day, the whole tribe of garbage pickers knew that. But Paul's vision was quick and clear — the train would come that morning.

This was how the ideas of the future came to him. The ideas about the past were different, Paul needed his eyes for them. He needed to absorb the moment in the heap — the wind blowing through his coarse smock, see the train on the track, or the word-signs sticking through the black bags before the radio dreams started.

Paul didn't know what to call the visions except radio dreams. He liked to fidget with car radios in the heap. It had to be the old ones with the numbered grid and red needle, not the sleek ones with the blank screen. But the only way to get them to work was with a battery taken from a new wreck. The East stopped sending cars on the train when Paul was a little boy so most batteries were half eaten from the acid. Paul liked hunting for a good battery and hooking it up in an old car. Then voices from far off would form a scene in Paul's mind, like a dream that came when he was sleeping. The radio talked about things he couldn't understand, places he would never see, and all he could do was listen, which was the way it was with his visions.

Samatron, the boss, hated finding newer batteries in old cars and he would always take them out, cursing Paul as he did. Samatron hated anything that changed, anything new. He was always shouting at Paul, but Paul guessed that having people angry with him was all part of being named after a poet.

Paul's mother had found his name on a book before he was born. Guessing some infection would overtake her after the birth, she insisted the women call her child Paul, boy or girl, healthy or sick.

Paul remembered the book, the black print, the yellowed paper that smelled faintly of smoke and sweat. On the cover, under the blackened title, was written *a book of poems* and Paul had come to understand that poems were a special way of talking, of telling a story or explaining life. Sometimes they made little sense to him and other times the words brought glowing images, causing Paul to believe that poems were a radio dream of words.

A voice called his name from the heap. "Paul, you're gonna be sorry. You're gonna be wishin' ya could keep yer mouth shut," the old woman said. "And wishin' the gar took ya home. That's fer sure."

"Go away, Crane. Your words are broken glass rattling in the tin cans of my ears."

"Paul, git outa there. I's talkin' to ya." Crane kicked at the rubber tire of his shelter. "I sayin' now for the tribe ta hear that there is four kinds of gar not just three."

"Go away. The maggots have crawled through your ears, into your skull."

"First, the gar da train wants. Den da nat'ral gar, you know. Da rain, sun, ground water. Third, dere's da tiny gar that causes 'fections, dat eats our flesh, turns us mad — "

" — mad like you."

"Then Samatron says to da tribe, dere's Paul, a gar unto his own." The old woman laughed. "You better run and hide. Samatron's coming and he's mad."

"Why is that new?"

"You shouldn't be reading. You know that makes him mad." Crane cocked her head so she could see down into the tunnel of the shelter. Paul saw her grey hair, her scaled face where one sunburn had layered over another. She had come from the East as a young woman, and liked to sing and tell stories about her past, but Paul knew she was making them up.

"Reading is the reward for the masters."

"There's no masters, only pickers and you'se gonna be sorry ya read. You should keep yer mouth shut," she said, and disappeared behind a rusting box spring.

Paul opened his eyes. Someone he had never seen before was leaning over him. The man had a clean face as if hair had never grown on it. Paul could see where his beard had been scraped off, and the skin was as smooth as a woman's. The man's clothes were sharp and crisp, made of a fine plastic, not at all like the coarse-spun gar-bags that Paul's long smock was made from.

"Get out of here! I'm sick of you damn vagrants scaring the paying customers away. No wonder this town is going to hell." The man was shaking him. "God, don't you care how you smell?"

He pushed the man aside and sat up. No old machines or buses, not even one row of rusting, crushed or beaten cars were parked anywhere. Nor were there green, black or orange gar-bags, only a clean, smooth ground that had been stamped down and painted with yellow lines. Paul went to the edge of the walkway to look down the path. It went on forever in both directions.

Though everything was straight and new, the wind moved through it in a familiar way. Paper wrappers rustled in the street. There were only a few days in Paul's life when such a current hadn't licked at his face — sometimes hot and dusty, picking up rust and trash in the heap, brushing grit into sunburnt shoulders, bare asses, sore eyes. Other times, the breeze was cold, fluid through the shelters at night as if the wind lived in Saskatchewan. Like the breath of all the pickers long dead, and the people before the garbage came.

"You're leaving, right?" The man was leaning up against a tall door, but it couldn't have been a shelter. It was like one of the structures filled with rats on the far edge of the heap, except that this place wasn't rotting. It was untouched by garbage, clean and brightly painted, no signs of vermin.

"Are you the Boss?" Paul asked.

"I am. This is my store." The man sighed heavily. "And trying to make a life for myself is damn hard because of people like you. You haven't any money, do you?"

"No," said Paul, wondering what he did have — a smock, some body lice, and maybe his sandals. He leaned forward and saw that, indeed, he did have sandals, and that under the dirt on his toes was skin just as pink as the man's face and hands. Paul thought it was good to have something in common.

"Why don't you get a job?" the man asked.

"I don't know what you mean."

"Your kind are always full of excuses. You probably didn't even go to school, did you?" The man looked down the pathway, then at a flat disk on his wrist that reminded Paul of the washers he picked along with the screws, nuts and nails.

"No, but I taught myself to read," Paul said, and smiled.

"Yeah. A regular self-made man, aren't you? Listen kid, take a hike. Important people are coming from Ottawa to look at my store and if you're standing here, there goes ten thousand right off the top."

"Is this the past?" Paul asked.

"We don't have enough to feed our own children without you transients coming off the train. You're probably heading down to Laurier for a meal." The man stepped away from the tall building to look down the path, then went into his store. Paul marvelled at the clean windows. Inside the shop, clothes hung from silver rods. The man had disappeared.

"Nice day, isn't it?" said another man, clothed as carefully as the store owner. He stopped before entering the building and handed Paul a piece of paper with a two, and an old but well-dressed woman on it.

Paul crouched in his cramped shelter, his heart pounding. He had never had a vision this long, with people talking to him. Something strange was happening, he thought, as he set his feet against the rounded sides of the tires. Maybe today would not be like all other days.

"Paul, I want to talk to you." Samatron stood outside Paul's shelter. The stench of diapers, spray cans, rust, oil, plastic was getting stronger with the heat.

Samatron had his usual morning face, grit in his eyes, dried spit on his cheeks. The Boss thought he was special because his mother had lived long enough to feed him her own milk. Even when they were small, playing with threshing machines and hiding in overturned oil drums while gar-rain contaminated the barren ground even more, Paul knew Samatron resented him.

Before Samatron could run to ask his sickly mother, the younger Paul would explain the mystery of gears, of words, the history of machines.

"Listen," he sighed. "I know you were talkin' ta Palliser and Polaris about that stake past the old cars that says *Vanhorn 1 km*. This morning Pella told me you wrote something like that on the train with chalk before it pulled out. I wanta know why, 'cause you never asked me anything about it." Most of the others thought Samatron was the only one who could read.

"As I told Pella we are Vanhorn 1 km — the shelters of wood and brick we find falling to dust past the tracks where the old ones used to live. Those people in the East have records. When the train gets there from Saskatchewan they'll know exactly where the garbage came from."

"I mean, who told ya that pole means this is Vanhorn 1 km?"

"Samatron, must I say it again and again? No one tells me anything. Crane throws a ball at Dole and he doesn't expect it, but he lifts his arms to react. It's like that."

"One of yer so-called radio dreams, right?" Samatron asked. "Come off it, Paul. I'm sick of yer stories, and tellin' the women to go live in the old cars when they have a baby . . . "

"The old cars are cleaner than any rotten corner here. The mothers lie in the dirt and contaminated water. No wonder we haven't had a baby live since Dole. This tribe will die."

"Not that yer trying ta bring more young ones into the tribe. Or don't you want a woman? You scare 'em away talkin' about the past." Samatron spit. "Just keep yer radio dreams to yerself."

Paul did not look at Samatron, but let his eyes drift to the gar-heap piled past his shelter. "Doesn't it make you mad, too? Remember when we were small? The garbage coming on the train for years. Cars, Oscars, GE's, plastic, glass. Unending, unquestionable, unstoppable, unwanted, useless, stinking and rotting."

"They didn't know what to do with it."

"So the East sent it here to forget about it?"

"You think too much, Paul. Ya gotta jus' let 'er go. That's what gets me about you. Pella and I know what we are. We're happy ta pick the gar, eat the food and not wonder too much about anything, not the days before, or the days ta come. That's why we got no use for yer fancy talk or yer damn dreaming."

"Samatron, if you want, I'll tell only you. No one else has to know." Paul paused. He had told Samatron so many of his visions that he hesitated to bother again. "Today, this morning, the train will come."

"I know that."

"You're only guessing. Why not tell the others if you know for sure?" Paul asked.

"'Cause then they won't work as hard. They'll stand around all morning claimin' they can't eat those last few withered potatoes. A whole morning of pickin' would be wasted waitin' for the train." Samatron stepped toward Paul. "No one cares about yer stupid dreams anyway."

"But you do! You know I've been right many times."

"Sometimes ya guess and yer right. Who cares? Yer makin' things harder for everyone with yer big mouth."

"But I'm not. If you just listen to me, I could help. Don't be so frightened this tribe will abandon you if you try something new and fail."

"Listen, ya sewer-picking rat, if you talk anymore about yer rotting dreams, that's it! You'll have ta go, one way or another." Samatron turned and walked away, finding a path through the garbage.

Paul folded his arms across his chest and leaned back against the shelter, feeling the hot rubber through his black smock.

2

The wind had a way of coming up in the night, howling like a mad woman, rattling the metal scraps against the hoods of tractors and trucks. It scattered magazine pages over the whole heap. Paul was used to it and he expected it. Though he hoped many things would change, he knew nothing could be done about the wind. // today

It had no purpose, Paul thought. It came and went without reason. The moving air was empty except for bits of rubbish. It resembled a voice crying out, but for what? Paul didn't know why the wind bothered him so much.

But the women paid it no heed, and picked a place near Paul's shelter to clear debris.

Not that they were clearing the space for anything special. Long ago, Paul asked Samatron if the tribe could plan new shelters, working on them only when the sun was too hot to gather items for the train. That spot would have been perfect for the project. Samatron said no. No time.

Paul couldn't understand why the women kept coming back to sort through the trash. Perhaps just to feel the once-fertile soil in their childless hands. Maybe to give Dole a place to play. But whenever they picked that spot, the night wind would fill it with garbage again.

Paul looked at the heap — the dry, oily dirt under the scraps of plastic wrappers and trash. For a minute, a shaded green was all he saw, then the barren space came back to him.

Green stretched before Paul like a great sheet of smock cloth. He wondered if anyone could ever step on that ground; it rippled with the ever-present wind. Not smooth and painted like the pathways from his other dream, but hilly and rolling, shadowed and bright. In the grass children played with a red ball, laughing and tossing it to each other, away from some, on to the next, a frolic unknown in Paul's memories.

Paul studied them. Although they weren't as clean and neat as the man with the store, the children were healthy and well-fed. One of the little girls had dark skin and rows of frizzy brown hair. Her smile lacked a tooth in the front of her mouth and she waved to him. Paul waved back.

Behind the children, a wall of jutting lines and billowing fragments swayed in the fragrant breeze. Crane, the old woman, said there were trees in the East, and Paul gasped when he followed them up into the sky. How could something grow so tall and not have any bolts or an iron framework, not even cables to keep them upright?

All his other dreams were like peeking in a dirty window. Even pictures in rotting magazines that had bothered Paul before were not as real as what he saw then. If Samatron could have been there to see the clean land, the young children playing in open spaces, their clothes, the green that just seemed to grow, then he might have known what the tribe could work for. That in time, with hard work and a little sun, the tiny area the women picked could be something special.

Not far from Paul, two men in yellow suits stopped their yellow truck. On the doors were the words City Works. Crane had once rambled on when she was sick saying the Eastern Authorities threw anyone they thought was poor or crazy on the train. That was how she came to Saskatchewan. Had these men come to get someone like that?

At a corner where the compressed roadway elevated, one of the men removed an axe out of a brown case while the other watched. The sound of hacking echoed down the street as if it came from everywhere, as if it was too big for such a small, thin target.

"Don't!" Paul said, wanting to pry the little tree out of their hands.

He wanted them to see inside his head — the oil-black dirt, the bags, broken chairs, rusting cars, spray cans, the trash that went on forever. He needed them to see a place that knew no trees other than the one Crane had formed for Dole from shreds of plastic pinned to the ends of wire coat hangers.

"Get lost, you bum," said one of the men, not angry, not fierce, but in a light whisper, as if Paul wasn't worth the energy shouting used. The man tossed the branch into the back of the truck, then they got in and drove away.

It had been a cold night. Paul wished there were more women, one for every man, not just two or three to share Samatron's shelter when he wanted. Paul longed for someone to press against, to feel her soft skin, listen to her breathing, keep her warm. He wished there was someone he could talk to about this vision.

Paul didn't know how to get the tribe to accept his dreams. It was a gift, like when Dole was born, but gifts could be taken away. Dole could die, like all the other babies, like Cassi who had died a day after Dole came. Paul's gift could be erased, too, if he didn't value it.

3

*P*aul crawled out from under a truck where he was removing a bumper. The rest of the men, all nine of them, were jumping on a thick pole to lever up a car. Paul suspected Samatron gave him this job because the bumpers were heavy. Sometimes they slipped before the bolts were out, and crashed to the ground. Paul had to jump out of the way or he'd be taking the train home. The men always said that, *Take the train home*, referring to the way the tribe sealed dead bodies in clear plastic bags to set on the train. When Samatron said it to Paul the men laughed.

"Get out of the way!" shouted one of them. Something heaved and the pole they stood on started to crack. Paul saw an older man slip and fall to the ground. No one was hurt but the machine still hadn't budged.

Then it came to Paul that one of the older wrecks not far away had a tall boom. *Towtruck* was painted on its dull purple side. In the past it would have lifted a car with the push of a button, but Paul thought the men could pull the cables by hand.

"Hey, Samatron," Paul yelled. "Why don't we move over the towtruck?"

"What ya babbling about? Can't ya see we're busy?"

"See this truck?" Paul said, pointing through the cars, past a rusty combine. "The cables aren't rotten. The tires haven't sunk into the soil. We took out the engine, so it's light. We could move it over to your wreck and ease it up."

"How?" asked one of the men.

"With these cables. We would attach the hook, put a pipe on this crank so we could all turn it. The wreck would be raised, then we could roll some drums underneath it and you men could get to work."

"Right, Paul," Samatron said, shaking his head. "We spend all afternoon draggin' yer truck over here, then all tomorrow hoistin' the cables up, and the wreck still won't give. Quit wastin' our time."

"Probably one of his looney dreams, where we is all standin' round with our fingers up our ass," another man said.

"Better not be," Samatron said. Paul tried not to hear the men laughing, but their words made his face redden. He wanted to push the truck over to the wreck himself, and show them he was right.

"Take the oil ta Moen, Paul. Make yerself busy," Samatron yelled as the men stood around arguing. Paul walked back and pulled the pail from under the great truck with KEN ORTH written across the grating, a faint shadow to show where a W had once been. Moen wouldn't need much oil to cook with anyway since the food supply was almost gone.

"Do I roast dese rodden dings?" she said, pointing to a few shrunken potatoes when Paul set the oil down. Gar had eaten the inside of her mouth, leaving fragments of white-turning-black teeth and a thick, dark tongue.

"No, the train should be coming now. I'll help get the flame going," Paul said. Moen smiled, and sometimes when he saw her mouth he wished he could do something. In the past, people studied books and would have known how to treat this kind of disease. All the tribe had now was Crane with her memories.

Paul remembered how Crane had once given a young man a drink of water mixed with oil. He'd had an infection from a cut on his head, and everyone thought he'd die. Crane said the turtle film of colours on the water would cure him. The man didn't die, which convinced the tribe that Crane's memories were worthy of their trust, but Paul knew that the oil and gas in the tanks was poison.

The cooking flame was burning as high as Moen and Paul's knees when the faint rhythm of the train could be heard. The tribe climbed out from behind their gar-bags and old cars to gather by the track. Everyone was hungry and tired. They had been eating oatmeal and potatoes for the last few days and were ready for the food the train brought. Samatron would be anxious to read the Book to see what the tribe would be collecting next. Copper, plastic and glass, the things that were always wanted lay piled by the track ready to be loaded into boxes.

The East used the Book to inform the tribe. Sometimes the train needed more glass than usual — maybe two crates instead of one. Maybe cast iron was in demand now. Samatron liked his merchandise to be the best quality possible. He urged his pickers to find as much as they could, to fill the crates with balls of green, black or orange gar-bags, or sticks of wire stripped clean of their cracked plastic coating. The Book told them how to put dead bodies on the train, and it had a page for Samatron to detail anything the tribe needed, like cooking pots or diapers for when Dole had been a baby.

As the train neared, Paul pictured Saskatchewan in the past when only a few people lived there. In his mind he saw dream-trains rolling down new track, bringing food and clothes for the people who worked the land. Paul didn't think they took garbage then, but something else. He didn't know the name. It looked like oatmeal, but this grain glowed like copper beads.

The engine car rocked to a stop. Paul studied it as always. The engine had no crate, just an empty seat and some controls that he could see only if he climbed up and peeked through the dirty glass. As a child he had done this all the time, fascinated by a seat that no one sat in, by buttons no one touched. Yet the engine knew exactly what to do — when to stop, and at what time it should retreat down the track back to the East.

Pella, with help from the boy, Dole, loaded plastic into the crate that Samatron had marked for it. The men filled another crate with copper while the old women struggled to get food out of the second car. Moen's black smile flashed over every box she handed to Maggie below her. Maggie wanted a new smock and would get one if Samatron wrote it down in the Book.

China's job, which was to load glass, needed careful hands. Paul knew China was smart and he also liked the way she chopped off her red hair so it stuck up in short tufts while everyone else's was long and tangled. Late one night, Paul had wondered if China was the woman for him. Everyone else had left for their shelters and China's eyes had caught the oil flame, like a car mirror catches the sun, beaming it back at Paul. The wind was especially cold that night, and they huddled close to the flame, almost touching. Paul thought she liked him, his stories, his questions about the past. He went to sleep dreaming about her, but the next day she mocked him in front of Samatron.

He'd had a vision about her having a baby once which he thought couldn't be true since China wasn't big-bellied or sick. Her friend Cassi had died so quickly after Dole came. But this time China's baby died. When Paul saw her sitting by the fire all alone, he wanted to tell her he had no dreams that she would die, too. But he couldn't bring himself to say anything. She didn't put the body on the train, but gently laid the black bundle in a hole by a flat stone that had been set in the earth from times before.

Then something occurred to Paul. He ran past Samatron to the crate behind the engine.

"The East put this white container back on the train," Paul said, holding it up. Samatron shook his head, and from the tribe's faces Paul could tell they didn't remember.

"What are you talking about?" yelled Palliser, tossing pipe up into a crate.

"The one the women discovered that Samatron said to put on the train," Paul told him. It was just the way the tribe found it except the cap had been taped on with thick, sticky plastic. It looked like one of the water jugs from the train, but inside was something Paul could only guess at.

"There's a note about it in the book," Samatron said. "*Please leave the med-I-cal container in the landfill. Do not open. Very dan-gerous.* Know any songs about medical, Crane?"

She shook her head. "Doctor," she said, then, "Sick people." Her body rocked from side to side like it always did when she was trying to remember.

"Sick?" Samatron echoed. "Then throw it back in the heap like the Book says." He grabbed the jug from Paul. Inside the white plastic a black line had settled, like something had dried there. Paul thought hard about the line, but the visions only came when he didn't force them.

"I wonder what those are?" Samatron was referring to the rattling objects inside the jug. "Maybe we could open it anyway. Them people in the East don't know everything."

"No!" shouted Pella. "If the book says not to, then leave it alone."

"Why, are ya frightened, Pella?" Samatron asked, a cocky grin on his face. "It's a curious thing."

Paul hated when Samatron said this because Samatron wasn't curious at all. He wanted to show the tribe he had the power and courage the rest of them lacked. Samatron picked at the tape but Paul could see that it had fused together over the cap, becoming a solid plastic ring.

"Just leave the damn thing. It's 'taminated. Shit, Samatron, you jez gotta get your hands into everything. If they says to leave it in the heap, then do it." It was Prusha, a plastic picker. Some of the tribe went back to filling crates and Moen hobbled off with her food.

"Wished ya didn't have ta show the whole damn tribe that jug." Samatron spit and walked away.

***

The high sun made everyone silent and lazy at the midday meal. After a bowl of thick soup, Moen handed each of the tribe a long black thing to eat. The outside was tough and rubbery with cracks that let flies in to lay their eggs. Paul oozed the sweet yellow cream onto his tongue. Pella didn't like hers so she gave it to Dole, who was sitting outside the circle of pickers.

"Looks too hot to work this afternoon, Samatron," said Polaris. She threw one of the dark skins into the flame. It sizzled and the heavy smoke coiled in the air. "Samatron?"

"Yeah."

"Sky looks too clear to work. The sun's getting a bugger."

"Yeah." Samatron stretched and yawned, though his eyes weren't at all heavy with sleep.

"What do you think we should do with that jug, Samatron?" China asked.

"Throw it in the heap, I guess."

"But they said it was dangerous."

"Why do we need to do anything with it?" asked Makita, who had limped since he was boy when a car crushed his knee. Samatron often listened to anything Makita had to say, probably because he never felt that this man could ever gain power over him.

"It's jus' a jug," Samatron said. His eyes drifted to the train, to the car behind the engine where all the dead bodies had been placed — their mother's, Cassi's and the old mens'.

"No, we gotta do more than that," Prusha said. "For Dole. If the East sends it back here like that it must be bad gar."

"So's everythin' else around here. Lots of things the train hasn't asked for. Like them damn shitty diapers we find. We just leave 'em in the heap, slip on their slime, fall on our asses. It's just a jug. Why are we botherin' so much with it?" Samatron asked.

"I just wish I knew what kinda garbage it really was," China said, scratching her head. "What if Dole does open it?"

"Maybe there's somethin' good about it? Somethin' we don't know," Samatron answered.

All China did was set a black skin from her dinner in the flame.

Then the whole tribe was quiet which Paul hated. He knew he was right about the train, and so many other things, but never in a bolt's life of rusting would they or Samatron ask him if he knew any more. It was like he wasn't there. Right then he didn't know what the container was about, but he would. His dreams would come to help them.

"Yes we have no bananas!" Crane shouted behind Paul, singing it over and over. It must have been a song from her past and she would rant it until the still meaningless words followed Paul into sleep.

"Yes we have no bananas."

4

No clouds shaded the heap, but a light haze lay above it like a thin blanket.

Everyone except Paul was in their shelters sleeping or thinking. He, in the semi-darkness of a car, guessed that Samatron was probably rubbing his bare legs against another woman. Maybe it was Pella or Avon making him hot and sweaty that afternoon. Samatron put as much effort into trying to get Pella on her hands and knees in his shelter as it took to strip combine gears. She was about as stubborn too.

Paul sat pushing the black buttons of a radio, sending a red needle up and down the numbered grid in hope that sounds would come from the dashboard. An oily film covered the windows making the hideaway almost perfect for thinking and dreaming.

Paul had never known his mother, and the tribe's old people couldn't remember much. She lived only a day or two after he was born. Maybe she was like him, things came to her from the air and she had no one to tell.

Or maybe Paul's father had had radio dreams. His parent's parents might have been two of the old people who lived in Saskatchewan before the garbage was shipped. Before the last of the schoolers left for cleaner air, and before the crimers climbed off trains from eastern prisons.

He liked to think his ancestral mother's hair was long and yellow, her arms strong. That there was no dirt in the pores on her nose, her toes were straight and clean. Her mate might have looked like Paul, hair matted with grime from working on farm machinery all day, making the engines run rather than tearing them apart for salvage. When each long day was through, the father would have returned to hold the mother close in their ancient bed until cold dark came and made the fine hairs on their backs lift.

Paul wondered if his mother had held him after he was born. Sometimes when he saw Crane cuddle Dole he knew that's what mothers were supposed to do. If Paul ever had a woman he wanted her to understand the ideas that came to him. She would want to sit in the old cars after the birth, cradle the babies, give them milk from her tits, keep them warm.

Paul punched the black buttons again with his finger. This radio had worked before, but now no sounds came. His arms were red from that morning, and he scratched a scab above his elbow.

Then it hit him. The line on the bottom of the jug was blood. It dripped from the other things he could see in his mind. About fifty sharp, long metals — *needles* — were in the bottom of the jug. *The blood came from people's arms.* Paul could see people lining up, and then he saw the bloodied needles dropped into the jug.

But this didn't make any sense. Why was the jug so dangerous, he wondered? Blood was only blood, wasn't it? Or maybe it was that the needles were dangerous. But the tribe handled glass and fine wires all the time. This was how it was with his dreams; they didn't explain themselves. Paul was given a piece of information, but not everything. He was always left with questions to think about. One thing was sure, though. Blood couldn't eat through the plastic like an acid. It wasn't a skull and boner, or gar-bleach.

Paul took a deep breath. The air in the car was thick and old, and he felt sleepy. The radio hadn't made any sounds — he would have to put water in the battery. There would be no woman for him this afternoon, no radio sounds, just a few strange visions that made little sense. Paul lay down on the hard vinyl seats and closed his eyes.

***

Paul hated waking up in the afternoon heat, his face dirty, his belly a hard, hot ball. But the worst was his thirst. Paul spent his youth learning to ignore it. The train brought muddy, foul water which Paul drank only when he absolutely had to.

He swallowed hard, determined to do without a drink again. Instead, he wandered into the heap to think. He found Avon and Prusha picking the gar-bags.

Pella was not far away, bending over rubble. Her short smock was stiff and it stuck up at the back showing her dirty brown panties. Paul focussed on the red streak down the inside of Pella's thigh, and sighed. If Pella wasn't such a bitch all the time, dreaming about looking pretty, being like some of the women whose faces she saw in books — eyes bright and skin as if it was a painted mask — Paul could have liked her. They might have had a baby. But that would never be.

He knew he should get back to removing the bumper, but the women were gathered in a tight circle, and he wanted to know what had caught their attention.

"Find anything good?" Paul asked Prusha.

"Yeah," she said. "See this bag? Water and sun have never gotten in. See the paper? Blue. Shiny. Smooth." She squinted, and her red face reminded Paul of a crumpled brown bag. Paul squatted on his knees to look. Crushed paper balls were mixed with flat shiny strings, some wide, some narrow. Paul could smell how crisp and significant they had once been.

"I never saw anythin' like it. The others have, but it rots before I find out what they was talkin' about. Why would somethin' so pretty be stuffed into a bag and tossed away?"

"This paper used to cover boxes and . . . things. In the boxes I see appliances like we load onto the train sometimes." Paul's stomach tingled, his hands were shaking. "People are standing around tables, wearing . . . not smocks like us, but dressed in shiny, bright colours with sweeping bottoms." He smelled the hot fragrance of people. He heard their noises, the way they laughed, talked, sang and drank clear bubbly water from glass cups. Paul could no longer see Prusha, or the gar-bag filled with coloured paper. He could hear only the loud rhythms and heartbeats of beautiful men and women.

"Paul, what are ya doin'?" He heard a man's faint voice. "Paul, stand up. Now!" Someone grabbed him by the shoulders and the vision was replaced by strewn trash and shabby women. "What are ya talkin' about?"

"The paper." Paul pointed to the ground, trying to stop the images. He wasn't sure where he was, in the heap or by the boxes on the table. "Give me a glass of the bubbling water," Paul mumbled.

"You ass, I told ya what would happen if ya kept on with that!" Then Samatron slapped his face.

"I'm sorry, I couldn't stop it," Paul said, and he knew he was begging Samatron, something he hated to do but he was weak with bewilderment.

"I don't say words if I don't mean 'em. You got a choice, Paul. You can leave or starve. I ain't yer Boss anymore."

"It wasn't that bad, Samatron. We were just talking." Prusha put her hand on Samatron's arm as if to restrain him, but Samatron shook her off. Paul's forehead was dripping sweat, the energy of the dreams making his whole body hot.

Pella's dark eyes sparkled and she smiled, glad that Paul had gotten what was coming to him. Avon turned away, her face blank. Prusha's concern faded too. Paul saw the men in the old cars watching.

"What are ya gonna do?" Samatron asked.

"About what?" Suddenly he felt very tired.

"You staying and starving, or leaving?" Samatron asked.

"I don't know." Paul could do neither. He wished he never had the dreams. They seemed more a curse than a gift. It would be better if he was just like everyone else. As he stomped away to the old cars, a large piece of yellow plastic tumbled across his path. Paul kicked at it, but missed.

5

It wasn't the morning heat — though it was bad enough under the black rubber — that woke him up. It wasn't the oil smoke either, or the smell of burning potatoes, but the faint shouts and voices Paul didn't recognize. When he rolled out the end of his shelter his knees hit thick mud. He scrambled to get up, and though he hastily wiped the mud off with a scrap of plastic, his knees still stung. He had to be careful. Burns could get infected before they healed.

Paul was usually careful but he hadn't expected the mud since he didn't hear the rain during the night. He must have been sleeping very deeply, he thought.

Walking through the maze of rusty bed springs and washing machines Paul found the others sitting on sheetmetal around the flame. Two women wearing large hats stood among the tribe. Their skin was pale compared to everyone else's. Paul thought Samatron would start shouting as soon as he saw him but he didn't. A black-haired woman was talking while her shorter companion listened with the rest. Paul sat down.

"Don't open the jug." She was pleading with Samatron. "And stop arguing, we know you have one."

"What do you know about my tribe?" asked Samatron.

Paul suddenly realized he hadn't known these two were coming. He always knew when something unexpected would happen, but this was a surprise and he wasn't sure how he felt about it.

"I told you, your train passes through our heap," the black-haired woman was saying. Her face was slight and gentle and she talked differently than the Vanhorn tribe, like the words were forced out of her mouth.

The shorter woman had small eyes the colour of oil and a smile that reminded Paul of pictures the women sometimes found in the heap. *The Immaculate Heart woman* whose heart was as delicate as a fume on top of her chest. In the pictures the woman's lips curved slightly into a smile, but she didn't look happy. Paul had dreams about her too. People used to talk to her even after she was dead because she had a son who died in a special way. They believed she could hear them, so they mouthed silent words to her. Paul used to think that maybe he was a bit like her, receiving messages from the air.

The small woman looked at Paul and smiled.

"You saw the jug?" Samatron asked, bending forward to hand Paul a potato from the flame. Several people noticed, Prusha was one of them, but no one was as puzzled as Paul.

"One of our men was working on top of a derrick when the train came by. He remembers seeing it," said the one with the oil-coloured eyes.

"So what does this gotta do with us?"

"Well, a while ago, maybe fifty days or so — "

"As long as it takes paper to rot," interrupted the oil-eyed woman.

" — we found a container like that. We didn't send it on the train because I didn't think we needed to. The train has never asked for anything like that. But the children were playing with it and it was full of needles — "

"Needles?" interrupted Samatron.

"They're like thin, sharp nails. I had no mind one way or the other about it, and the mothers didn't say anything to the children so a couple of days went by. First it was a small baby, just learning to talk, who died." She stopped and Paul leaned closer to hear. "In seven days, all the children who played with the jug died. We found marks on their skin. Something about the needles must have killed them. That's why I'm here . . ."

"How many children?" asked China. Paul wanted to know himself, and how many mothers too. He wanted to ask her why their children and mothers lived.

"Six," said the oil-eyed woman. "How many do you have here?"

"One," said Palliser. He pointed to the shelter where Dole lay sleeping. The woman nodded.

"How did you know ours was the same type of container?" asked Samatron.

"I didn't. That's why I had a look at it."

"You had no right to just come over ta our train and look in our box," Samatron said. "I'm the Boss here. I handle the problems. And you aren't takin' the jug."

"It's yours," the oil-eyed woman said. "It was in your heap, your tribe found it. We've been thinking for some time now that we should come this way to meet you, then this happened. We wondered if you might want to bury that jug with ours."

"You can do what you want," said the other woman. "But what if your children find it when you're dead, or the tribe moves a bit, shifts in the heap, or loads on the other side of the track. Young kids come along or a new tribe wanders . . . "

"I think we should listen to her. Let's give them the jug," shouted Pella.

"Think about what you're doing, Pella. I wanna know how we can believe anything these women say?" Samatron was shaking. "She said they had six children. In all my life this village has never had six children. The most was four and that was me, Paul, Makita and Prusha. We was almost old enough to have babies ourself before Pella came.

"And how did they get here? Not from walking in the sun yesterday. I wonder if the whole tribe of them have come to steal food."

"Why would we want your food? We have food from our own train. See? Tins of soup and bananas." She pulled a spun-plastic bag from her shoulder.

"Bananas?" said Samatron taking a step closer to look. "Ya took that off the train when it passed. That's our food!"

"Oh, don't be stupid," said the black-haired woman. "Your train is moving when it passes us. We get the same food from the East that you do, that's all. We probably load the same stuff."

"Why don't you have more children?" asked the one with the oil-eyes. "Two or three of you seem the right age." She was looking at Pella, Avon and China. They wouldn't lift their heads. One of the old women who would only speak to Crane snickered.

"Never mind, lets talk about how ya got here." Samatron flapped his arms at the old woman to make the cackling stop but she kept right on. This made him more angry.

"But how is your village going to grow? Aren't you worried you'll die out?"

Paul wondered if the black-haired woman ever had a child. Maybe it had died from the jug.

"Forget it. It ain't yer tribe," Samatron said and turned to the pickers. "See, I told ya. How can we trust 'em when they tell us stories like that? Havin' six children and all."

"Oh, Samatron! Yer getting yer beard rolled into a ball," said Pella. "We never get visitors, and these women make me think."

"Exactly what I'm saying! They want you ta believe lies. Why else did they come here?" Samatron said.

Paul knew Samatron was afraid that the tribe would lose trust in him and listen to the others. It was the same reason Samatron wouldn't listen to Paul. Still, Paul didn't understand why Samatron had given him the potato. It wasn't like him to go against his word, especially in front of the others.

"These women show up from nowhere," Samatron continued. "They wanta take our container and you're all quick to nod. They tell ya a story about six of their tribe's children dying. Remember

Cassi? She was a strong one and still she took the train home. Others here tried having babies, too, but it's not easy. And we got good garbage. No gar-chemicals or pits that go down into the earth where a guy's gotta spend half his time climbing in and out."

Paul wished for a vision, something to show him how the other tribe lived.

"We'll do what we want. And we should all get ta work before the sun's a bugger, or maybe now ya want white skin like these women?" Samatron stomped away.

China motioned for the women to sit with them. "Stay. The boss is smart. He'll do the right thing in the end." The women sat down. "Do ya want a potato?"

"No, we don't want to burden you with our stomachs, too. We thought we'd do you a favour," one said. "I wish someone would have told us about the container before our children opened it."

"Are ya sure it was the needles?" asked Makita.

"It is the only thing we could think of. And we know they poked themselves when they played," said the oil-eyed woman. "You only have one child here? Who is the mother?"

"Cassi died when he was born. Sometimes the child dies, or maybe both," China answered. Paul could see that she was thinking about her own baby.

"I've forgotten your names," said China.

"I'm Braun, and she's Singer," said the black-haired woman.

"I'm China, this is Pella, Avon, Prusha." China introduced some of the others but left out the older ones, and Paul.

★ "So both of our tribes use names from the heap," said Singer.

"One village we heard of calls their babies after cars. Buick, Capri, Ford," said Braun.

"It must be a joke in the East when we record the newborns in the Book. *They got another little girl in Vanhorn 57 km, Rubber Maid,*" said Braun. The women laughed, and Pella looked at Paul.

"You have a sign by your tribe that says Vanhorn 57 km?" Paul asked. Were all the places in Saskatchewan named *Vanhorn something km?*

"We saw another one right before we found you. It said *Post 51*, right along the track. The heap gets so thick in places. It's piled as high, even higher than the train," said Braun.

"Any other signs?" Paul asked. Avon made a clicking sound with her mouth.

"Can't we talk about something else?" asked Pella, but Singer answered.

"No, just a couple *STOPs*, but the train never does." Paul was intrigued that even these two women called their heap by the sign that was outside it.

"That was for cars and machinery in the times before the garbage came," Paul said. "A train would be going too fast to stop."

"How do you know?" asked Singer.

"Anybody could think that up. Doesn't take a schooler or someone who got his mother's milk to know the cars had to stop for the train," said Makita in his deep and quiet voice. Some of the men had already left to work on the wreck, but Paul was watching the oil-eyed woman.

Everyone was quiet for a while, then Crane started humming and singing to herself, "*Big wheels rolling, gotta keep 'em going.*"

"So, you'll stay for a day?" asked Makita.

"Yes. We're always wondering about your tribe," said Braun. "Maybe we can learn from you, help each other out."

"*The white line is the life line to the nation,*" sang Crane.

"Samatron's all right. Sometimes he thinks someone will walk in this landfill and do a better job than he does," China said, and Pella nodded.

"Is your Boss like that?" asked Avon.

"I bet all Bosses are," said one of the old men. "They always are." The women looked at each other, then glanced in the direction the comment had come.

"I don't know. Am I, Singer?" Braun asked. "I've been leading our tribe for a while now, since the last Boss died."

The women nodded and smiled.

6

Since Samatron had handed Paul the potato it seemed he was back in the tribe, at least for a while. That meant there was work to do. The train needed scrap iron and sheetmetal, as always, so he started taking off more bumpers. Paul thought he should do this as payment for making them listen to his damn ramblings.

The oil-eyed woman was smart, Paul thought. Her slender waist was a shadow under her smock, and he imagined that her pale skin would feel like soft cloth to his touch. Paul had other questions for her, but he would wait until they were alone. He hoped that time would come.

***

When Paul worked by himself he liked to think of all he learned from his dreams. At times it was difficult knowing the difference between a vision like the one with the shiny paper and something that really happened. Others were not as clear and Paul couldn't remember if they were something someone told him, or just a guess. But the two dreams he'd had about the store and the tree were the strangest. He didn't know what he'd learned from them, if anything yet.

Though the gar-rain was quickly drying up, the ground was still sticky. Under the front of a large truck, Paul was careful to lie on sheetmetal. He heard steps in the mud, then Samatron's voice.

"Paul?"

At first Paul didn't want to answer. Samatron couldn't see him anyway, but he knew they had to talk. "I'm just loosening this bolt," Paul said.

In the dim light under the vehicle, Paul squinted at the rusting metal, the flaking chrome.

"What I said yesterday, Paul," Samatron paused, "I shouldn't have said. I think ya better stay."

"What?" Paul asked. "Then you understand that I couldn't help what happened?"

"I don't give a damn about yer gift. I just want the tribe ta work hard."

"Maybe I should go with the women. Their tribe might appreciate my dreams." This had just occurred to Paul. "Their tribe has children and women. They think about their lives and want to know about the past. I'd be useful to them. You should like that because if I went you'd have every woman in this tribe for yourself, to get on their hands and knees for you."

"I got every woman now," Samatron said.

"Yes, and I feel sorry for them. They scratch in the dirt their whole lives, never getting anywhere."

"What are you saying, then? You gonna go?"

"Why not? You don't want me here."

"I'm telling you to stay."

"It isn't like you to need something from me." Paul braced himself on the frame of the wreck, ready to push himself out, but stopped. "I know. You're afraid the rest of the tribe will go with me."

"I don't want ta open that jug, but you go with those women and I'll do it fer sure," Samatron said.

"That makes no sense."

"You don't want me ta open it, do ya?"

"No," Paul said. "You heard the women. It could kill, like it did their children. Think of Dole."

"But you'd be killing us if ya followed 'em back. Some of our people might go with you. There'd be nothin' left. Would ya want that?"

"What does it matter?" Paul asked, chipping away at some mud under the rim of the truck. "You're not doing much to keep them alive. How can you even think of opening that damn jug?"

"It's a curious thing — "

"I'm sick of you saying that!"

"If ya leave with 'em . . . " Samatron stopped. "No, the tribe wouldn't follow ya. Pella and China hate ya the most," Samatron said.

"Maybe, but they like the women," Paul said.

"How can you tell?" Samatron shouted.

"Don't be stupid," Paul answered. "Didn't you hear the way they were talking to them, the way they told you to shut up? Those women were right about one thing. If we don't have babies this tribe will die. And Pella, China, will listen and think that if they go to the other tribe they won't die having babies and their children will grow up strong and smart. No one will stay here with you." Paul wondered if Singer was alone too.

"I don't care. Go if you wanta and get yer gar-dreams somewhere else. Ya don't know that our women will go with 'em. They may never wanta have babies," he said.

"The black-haired woman, Braun, is the Boss of her tribe, you know."

"That one of yer *radio dreams*?" Samatron started to walk away.

"No, that's what she said."

"I'll tell her what a sore on my ass ya are. They won't want ya either," Samatron called as he disappeared behind the farm machinery. Paul knew Samatron could be right.

Paul grasped the wrench tightly, twisting a bolt. The threads were rusted together so he would have to try harder.

He cranked again, feeling his knuckles go numb. But instead of turning, the bolt crumbled. Fragments of metal and rust seemed to explode into his eyes. When he struggled to sit up, he hit his head on the inside of the bumper. Then, almost paralyzed by the shock, he fell back again and waited for the pain to recede.

"You all right?" a voice called as he pulled himself from under the truck. He recognized it as Singer's, the oil-eyed woman. Paul rocked back and forth, his hand on his forehead, his eyelid fluttering up and down like paper caught in the wind. Then her soft fingers were on his face, moving him to look into his eye.

"Yes. I just have to get the dust out."

"Should I bring some boiled water?" Her breath was warm on his face.

"Why?" Tiny bits of metal seared his eyeball like fire, and he wanted not to blink, but he couldn't stop.

"To clean it." She tried moving his hand away but he wouldn't let her.

"That will kill me for sure." Paul hated being sick. There was always the chance it would be his last time and he'd be taking the train home.

"Water is good if you boil it. Don't you know anything in this tribe?" Paul wished he could have seen her face right then, the lines in her forehead, her red lips, her brown eyes. "Sit still."

"The Book tells us all the time," Singer said as she wiped some of the dust from his cheeks, her touch so light, careful not to hurt him. "*Boil the water, keep the flies off the food, wash your hands after you pick.* Things like that."

"It's never said that in our Book. I'd know. The train tells you?"

"Always. If we want to know about something, we'll write it in the Book and they send back an answer."

Paul had questions to ask her but they didn't seem to matter right then.

"There, try opening them again." Paul did as Singer asked. "I only saw a flash of those green eyes of yours."

Paul's eyelids were squeezed shut. "I can't keep them open," he said.

"Well, I can understand that. I don't know if you can tell, but this one is cut."

"Great," Paul said, wishing the topic had less to do with his injury, and more to do with what else she might see. Singer was so close and Paul thought about how her words were whispered to him. He imagined the sounds she made were poems that took the shape of small winged creatures, not ugly like the flies that laid their eggs on the food, but delicate and dark mauve, the colour of the evening sky. He willed her words to brush his pain away, and he blocked out the reflex to blink so that he might see her face. When he did open his eye, it burned as if someone had touched it with an oil flame.

"I don't know what I'm going to do with this. I'll go get the old woman to prepare some water." Paul heard the rustle of her smock as she left, the plastic rubbing the back of her legs.

He could do nothing except sit on the sheetmetal, waiting. Here was Singer healthy, understanding, brave enough to walk down a track into the unknown, involved with important matters in her tribe, and Paul was the outcast in his own. He had nothing to impress her with. His fellow pickers silenced him at the flame, and he hadn't received any visions about the new women, or his accident.

If he had not hurt his eyes, he knew exactly what he would do. He would take off with these women, even follow them at a distance if he had to, sneak out of the tribe so the rest wouldn't know. He could have the new tribe all to himself and help Singer with whatever her job was in the heap.

Singer. He could just see her lying down with him, her warm skin a blanket against the night winds. Explaining the mysteries of childbirth, telling him the secrets of infections and the tiny garbage that resulted in night death. Singer might know how to read too. She might understand the magazines and rotting books in the heap. Maybe she had learned poetry, and could say the ancient word-patterns into the air, create pictures in their minds, stir up new impressions. When his eyes were fine he would get a radio working for her.

Paul walked on the compressed path. Hanging signs read Thompson, Bowell and Tupper. The pathway became dirtier and darker. Lines of trash cans overflowed, a smell all too familiar to him. No trees or grass grew along the powdery-grey walkways. No children were playing on the street. A rat scurried across the road and sat between two cans to chew whatever it had in its claws.

Huge shelters towered above him. He heard children fighting, babies crying. A woman sat on the ledge of a low window, hanging her head almost to her chest. He didn't know what to do or say, so he watched her.
"You looking for soup?" she asked. Her face was sunken, her eyes heavy.
"Maybe," Paul said.
"Won't do ya any good, dear." She lit a small tube on fire and lifted it to her mouth to suck. Paul guessed it was a new kind of food. She struggled to sit up.
"Is the wind always this cold?" He wrapped his arms around his body.
"Yup. Nothing to stop the wind on the prairies. You're gonna freeze your balls off. I betcha it's gonna rain, might even get frost tanight with fall only a month off," she said, looking down at Paul. "Maybe you'se gonna have ta steal pants off some poor bugger to keep warm."

Paul could see a red colour on her lips, and some grey streaks in her hair. He thought if she had a few days of sleep and work in a mild sun that she might not look so sad. But still, he would have rather been staring at Singer's face.
"You worried you might freeze?"

"Maybe," he said. Her legs were folded and her feet stuffed under her body. She blew white smoke out of her bright mouth and looked up.

"Aren't ya a man with lotsa words? If ya had money and a bath, little o' Cherry here might know where ya could sleep. And it would be warm, too," she said. Her eyes dipped again to look at Paul.

"Money. I don't know," Paul said, wondering what she was talking about.

"Yeah. 'Course no one has any money in Vanhorn," Cherry said.

"How did you know that's where I'm from?" Paul asked, fingering the paper in his pocket. "I should find that cooking place, though."

"I got beans, if ya want beans. Cooked 'em yesterday cause I found a ham bone in the barrels outside that ritzy cafe down on Ninth. I'm bettin' those beans ain't half bad. But you gotta have money."

"Well, I don't know. Like what?"

"Whatever ya got. I ain't too worried. God knows it's hard ta get any damn coin or trick these days."

"All I got is this," he said, holding the paper up to her.

"Ain't nothing wrong with that. Jus' how come ya got a two-dollar bill and no pants."

"I don't know," he said.

Inside, Paul saw a shelter like he had never seen before. He looked at and touched everything. Cherry rolled her eyes as Paul opened cupboards around the long tub and toilet. Some of the fixtures he recognized from the heap, and he'd had visions about how they worked, but now he needed to touch the clear water in the white bowl by his knees and smell the soapy water in the tub.

"I'll see if my old man left some shorts. Ya look pretty scrawny so I might have ta give ya some rope for a belt. Ain't doin' bad for two bucks. Must be your lucky day." She left and when she came back into the bathroom, Paul hadn't moved.

"Where I come from, there's no warm water, not trees or clean air. I've only seen birds once or twice when I was small."

"Birds," she said, raising her black eyes. "If you want birds, honey, jus' look above the door at the front here. There's a whole crop of 'em shitting on us all the time."

"And you have this place, this long bowl here to clean in."

"I sure can tell you ain't got any tubs in your neck of the woods. Be sure and wash your hair. And I'll see what I can do about that beard. It don't suit you. If ya were ta try and get a job, even loading the train, they wouldn't hire you with that." She pulled another tube from somewhere as Paul gathered up his smock. "See this cig? Guess how I get 'em."

Paul watched the red end crumble in a low fire inside the dirtied paper, and wondered what it would be like to suck on the end.

"Well, kid," Cherry said. "I used ta get the little bits of tobacco out of da butts in the street, but," she shook her head, "they weren't no good. Now I git 'em the same way I'm gitting your two bucks." She put the lid of the toilet down. Even with the crack in the seat, and the dirt and bugs on the green tiles around the tub, this place was cleaner than any shelter that he had been in.

"Ain't you gonna git in the water?" Cherry asked. "Even if I don't pay for the bloody stuff, I can tell you it ain't always easy gettin' in this bathroom. Her down the hall she's got seven little kids, poor bitch. All of them younger than ten, and always hollerin' and screamin'. Her old man leaves, comes and goes, gits pissed and finds work in B.C. The story of the century. Littlest of 'em has got something wrong with his belly and he screams all night.

"She used to use cloth diapers. She'd stand over this toilet washing out two or three buckets of these shitty diapers, and when a girl's gotta take a piss in the morning there ain't nothing worse. But she's got Pampers now. They smell up the garbage but sure's better than holding up the can!" Cherry sucked the rest of the fire out of the cig, and lifted the toilet lid to toss it in. Then she started coughing. Her face turned purple before she managed to quit.

Paul watched steam rise from the tub. He wondered how he was supposed to tell where the water was with all the bubbles floating on top. *After taking off his sandals, he lifted one foot to step in, but jerked it out.*

"It's hot."

"*Supposed to be hot, ya idiot.*" *She pulled a length of flimsy paper off a white roll, and blew her nose into it.* "*How's it gonna kill yer fleas? And take yer shoes off.*" *She pointed to his back.* "*How'd ya git all dose burns all over you? Ya weren't one of dose guys cleaning da PCB spill by da power plant, were ya?*"

"*No. This is from the sun. I never worked with chemical garbage. It's just sunburn.*"

"*Oh, dat's good. I heard ya can git cancer of the cervix jus' from doing dose guys.*"

***

When Cherry leaned over Paul, her smoky, greying hair hung in his face.

In the almost total darkness of her orange-and-mold-scented room, on the softest bed Paul ever had been in, he could touch and feel any part of Cherry's body, and he did with little hesitation and no instruction. She ran her rough lips where his beard had once been, stinging his sensitive skin. Her strong hands stroked the back of his head, the top of his thighs, his flat stomach.

Paul had always imagined how a woman's body would feel, and now his calloused fingers could seek out the unknown, the mysterious. Cherry's mouth wanted to suck at his but he turned his head. He watched as she balanced herself on top of him, gasping and gripping his hands so she could sway, slowly at first, then Paul joined the rhythm and made it quicker.

He closed his eyes, shutting out the darkness, making a vision of another woman in a new dark. Her face was softer than the one he touched, her legs stronger over his thighs. Her long hair brushed his chest. As the movements became stronger, more final, Paul tried to think of something to say but there wasn't anything he could have whispered to change Cherry into Singer.

Paul knew this strange, sickly woman was only doing what she did for the piece of paper he had given her. This made him wonder how important that paper was and what else could be done with it.

When the groaning and sweating was over and Cherry had turned over to stub out her cigarette and press against Paul's thin chest, he wondered what it would be like to lie with Cherry every night. He could sleep in her soft bed, wash in her tub down the hall, eat the beans or rice or carrots that he had seen in her fridge or watch the world underneath the window to the street where working motors powered cars and truck.

But he really longed for Singer.

7

When Paul woke he knew he was back in the heap, his eyes shut tight because of the rusty powder, the sun strong on his face. The dream had vanished and Paul felt slightly refreshed, as if a day had passed and he had slept well.

What did it mean? Paul was thinking about Singer when it started, and he had dreamt about another woman, a woman he wouldn't even want.

He sat back and tried to put the dream out of his mind. Injuries made him especially angry. He did what he was told to do — remove bolts, rip sheetmetal off oil tanks, or help to heave engines out of cars. Sometimes he smashed his knuckles and they bled like a woman. Or a guy would scrape his leg on rusty iron sheeting and the wound swelled like a potato in the flame.

The old men who collected the tin cans sometimes cut themselves on the lids. Sure as the sun they'd be dead the next morning. For a while the tribe stopped picking tin cans; it was best to just leave them and ignore the Book. Any little cut was an opening for the gar to get into their bodies, to make them hot and dreamy, and take their life away.

Paul had seen it many times but there was no way of keeping the gar out, no thick cloth that moulded to their hands, no extraordinary sandals that covered the top of their feet, their ankles.

Paul had once had a vision that in the past people used to wear glass windows over their eyes. Even now, one of the garbage pickers would find plastic eye-windows in the heap, but they wouldn't stay on. He thought there were pieces that twisted around the ears, but had rotted off. Something like that would have kept the dust out of his eyes.

Usually he was careful, but today he'd had other things on his mind. Like Samatron, and the way this morning had gone with the women arriving, and these visions that seemed to lift him right out of the heap and place him in another world. Paul thought about that other world. Cherry said something about the wind, about Vanhorn, that made Paul wonder. Maybe he was wrong about the sign in the heap, but he had never been wrong in a vision before. If it was the East, what did that mean? That he was *going* to the East? Was this what would happen to him if he lost his sight? Would he be thrown aboard the train to find the street, the trees, the woman with the cig?

Paul heard someone approaching but couldn't open his eyes.

"I let the water cool. That's what took me so long. And Crane here found this old cotton in a bag. We boiled it too, so I think it will be all right." Paul felt Singer's hand pressing the warm cloth into his face, dabbing at his eyes, dripping water on his chest.

"Rust has fallen in it before. All kinds of contamination but never this bad."

"Be all right." It was Crane. "God, look at it bleed. *Mend his crown with vinegar and brown paper*," she sang.

"I don't think it's blood, just rust water," Singer said, ringing the cloth into the pail. "You don't have much here, do you? We get more off the train than you."

"What do you mean?" Paul asked her. "What else do you get?"

"Cotton, gauze. Alcohol."

"Those words mean nothing to me."

"Well, the train sends us things like suncream. In the book it says *Apply to skin for protection from harmful rays*. Then we'll be asked how it worked, if we burned as bad, if it bothered our skin, that sort of stuff."

"The train gives us food and water and smocks, that's about it." Paul squinted, thinking past the pain so he might open his eyes just a little. Singer's face was there, close to his, shading him like a combine on a hot day. He wanted to reach out and feel her smooth skin, touch her brown hair.

"I can't understand that. Why not tell you what it tells us?" She was wrapping coarse, smock-like material around his head now. The warmth of the sun left his face as she did, and the light faded into darkness.

"Better ask Samatron. Or better yet, don't tell him anything."

"He's touchy about people questioning him, isn't he?" Paul reached up to feel the bandage around his eyes.

"It should stay on," she said.

"I'll just tie it. Where's that string?" Singer asked. Paul pictured her nimble movements, her confident poised lips as she worked on the wrap. He was almost sad she was finished.

"When I was just a girl, this man from another tribe called *Regina* came because he had been kicked out for fighting or something. I didn't understand that part. Anyway he worked with us for a while. He said that his tribe cleaned up a refinery site. You know, filled huge plastic drums with dirt and oil, then loaded the drums on the train. Anyway the train sent them pills — "

"What are pills?"

"Got an ill, take a pill," sang Crane.

"Little stones, the size of a fingernail. You swallow them and they do things in your body, make you stronger, take away the headaches, the blurry sight that sometimes happens when men work with chemical garbage. They're like food but different. The man said the train would ask if this made the tribe people feel better because the garbage they moved was so bad. He said the sour air made their eyes red, their throats sore. His hands were just awful where he had held the dirt, melted fingers with bubbles of bright red under the skin."

"And did the pills help?"

"He said that not all the tribe was supposed to take the pills. Some weren't supposed to take anything, and some of the older ones wouldn't touch a pill. They said they were poison worse than garbage. And sometimes those that took the pills died."

"From the garbage?" Paul asked.

"He thought it was from the pills. Like the people in the East were trying to see what would work, and what wouldn't." Her voice was soft and he felt a strange energy grow inside his stomach. Here was someone who thought about things. She had experiences he would find interesting, things he wouldn't know about if she never told him. And she was right here in front of him. If he reached up and touched her soft hair, her skin under her orange smock, he could feel that warmth inside her body and know she was real, alive.

Yesterday he knew nothing. He hadn't even dreamt about her, but she was here now, talking to him, brushing against his shoulder, sitting with him. And he wanted her. When he was better, he would follow her to the other tribe, and he'd wash his face more, keep his hair clean, rinse his mouth. He'd smile at her, tell her about his ideas from the past and she'd like him, maybe more.

"Well, I'm done with you now," Singer said. She paused and gave a final tug on the cloth. Paul could hear the sheetmetal creak when she stepped back. "Why don't you go lie down and rest?" Her voice moved so Paul knew she had stood up. He struggled to do the same.

"I'll help you to your shelter, Paul."

"Take me to the old cars, away from the garbage and mud." Paul held his arms to her, feeling for her cheeks, her smooth jaw, but it wasn't a young face against his fingertips, but that of an old woman.

"That's a good idea. Later I'll boil more water and clean the injury again." Singer sounded farther away while Crane's old strong arms led him off to a van.

8

"Paul, Paul, yer all right. Just sit still while Singer cleans yer face."

"No!"

"If ya don't sit still, she won't be able to change the covering, damn it." It was Pella's voice. Her body was pressed against Paul, and her arms held his hands down. "Maybe we should get Polaris. He's strong. He could handle Paul."

"There's battery acid on my face?"

"It's the infection. It's bad. I saw the Boss over there," said a soft voice to his left. "Why not call him to help? If we don't get this cleaned, he'll lose his sight for sure." Paul didn't know who she was.

"Samatron won't come to help Paul," said Pella. "Just sit still."

"Samatron heard you women talking about leaving his tribe and going with us. Is that what you're thinking of doing?" asked the woman's voice. Paul tried to remember what was happening. Why was Samatron so upset?

"Here, Paul. Have a drink of water." A cup was held up to his mouth.

"I never drink the water." Paul pushed it away. "I am Paul, seer of the future," Paul shouted. "Speaker for the past, named after a poet."

"What's he talking about?" asked the woman's voice.

"I am a garbage picker in the Landfill called Saskatchewan. Today, I will touch the garbage of the dead. I am Paul!"

"Paul, you'll have to drink it. You have to eat something. You're weak and you've been screaming all night." The voice was Singer's.

"Bring a torch so I can see. Where are the lights? You can't do this in the dark," Paul said. "Singer, bring a torch, bring some light. Singer!"

***

"How are you feeling, Paul?" Paul tried to lift his head.

"What do you want? Why won't you take these rags off my eyes." He squirmed to sit up but felt dizzy and unsure of where the bench seat ended and where the van's floor started.

"You've been dreaming for the last few days. Whenever we take off the wrap, you can't see anything anyway. At least it will keep the germs out." He recognized Singer's voice.

"Who are the germs? And what do you mean that I can't see anything. I have to see! You've been making me drink that damn water again! And what if I never see again? How am I going to leave?"

"You don't have to go anywhere. Just rest so you have the energy to get better."

"No, you don't understand. Samatron doesn't want me here. We're always fighting."

"He has enough problems without you threatening to leave too," she said.

"You, you're Singer?" Paul was forgetting what she looked like. Her voice sounded so natural and usual he had forgotten that she came to the tribe a few days ago. "I want to touch your face. I have to."

"Yes, just stay still. Or maybe you should sit up and come to the edge here, out the back doors. The fresh air might help. You might feel better." Paul felt her hand on his ribs and this made him shiver. A woman had never touched him in such a way — but of course they had. Hadn't Crane helped him to the van when his eyes were first hurt? Then what was it? Singer's smell, not sour and moldy like all the rest, but fresh and new, like she was a person from one of his visions. Maybe he was thinking about those children in her village, how so many had been born, that their mothers hadn't died at birth.

"My throat is so sore."

"It's all the yelling you've been doing. Every time we change your bandages, you scream and shout something terrible."

Paul's feet dangled off the edge of the van, and although he could smell the garbage and feel the sun on his skin, he knew he was missing something by not seeing Singer. And he didn't want to imagine what she saw when she looked at him.

"Just wait, Paul." Singer was so calm Paul was sure she didn't care about him. "You should all have real shelters to lie in. Not tires or vans."

"I know what is going to happen and so do you. You've lived in the heap long enough, or don't strong men in your tribe die?"

"Look, I could just leave now. Don't you care that I haven't? You're getting better. Your sight will be fine."

"You don't know anything about me, Singer. I'm different from the rest of them. The morning that you and that woman boss of yours came, I was supposed to go."

"Go where? I've talked to the other women. This is where the last train stops. No others pass through here, so you're hidden from the rest of Saskatchewan. You probably never guessed there was a tribe just a day's walk up the track."

"I'm tired of talking about it."

"Then do something to change this place."

"Change? No one here wants to change anything. That's my point. I don't care any more, either."

"Then why am I changing your bandage six times a day? If you want to die, go ahead. You're no different from the rest of us. And if you don't want to get better I won't waste anymore time boiling shitty water to clean your eyes."

"But you aren't listening. I am different. Dying might be the right thing for me." Paul thought of the Immaculate Heart woman and all the people who talked to her.

"You're talking crazy again. How are you so different?" Singer asked.

"I get ideas. Pictures in my head of the past. What it must have been like then. What people wore, and did, and smelled like. Radio dreams, because the ideas come out of the air, and I'm just like a radio playing them out loud. Some of the ideas are of what will happen in the future too. Like I knew the train was coming back the other morning."

Paul wasn't sure he wanted to tell her now. He felt so bad about his eyes, his complaining, he wondered if telling her about his gift would turn her away for good. "I know what those needles were used for."

"What?"

"They went into people's arms to remove blood. Like siphoning gas out of a tank."

"Why did they kill the children then?"

"I don't know. That's all I saw," Paul said.

"I can't see how you guessing at those needles makes you any better than the rest of us. We all wonder at the past. If you did something with what you know, that would make you different."

"You're just like Pella, Samatron and the rest. You don't believe me, but it doesn't matter. Samatron will let me starve to death and ship my rotting body to the East because I can't see."

"It doesn't just take eyes to make a difference. But you can't keep wishing you weren't here."

"I do wish I wasn't here."

"Then there's no sense in wasting my time talking to you, is there? The women have questions. Braun and I should think about going back to our own tribe. They'll be waiting for us."

Paul didn't move, didn't even let his feet swing. He tried not to think of anything until a numbness filled his whole mind, filled the space where his sight had been. He let this quiet grip him, unable to even feel the throbbing pain in his eye.

"I thought there was something quick and decided about you. I was watching. You were watching me too. But I don't care now, either. You can find your own way back to bed." Paul felt her weight shift from the edge of the van and then he was alone.

There was nothing Paul could think about without returning to question his vision. He wished he could escape, go somewhere else out of the heap, away from the mess, away from women who could leave him and not come back.

The soup line on Laurier Street was long enough to convince Paul that the people had slept there all night. His pants felt different, though he had worn pants before. Paul didn't smell any oil flame, or see a stove or burner anywhere. No one was moving forward either.

Men, but also some older women who reminded Paul of Crane or Moen, were leaning or sitting up against the side of the building, under a sign, Salvation Army Soup Kitchen. *Some of the men were clean, no beards or dirt on their morning faces, while others looked like they had just come from the landfill sites.*

"So where's the heap? Or are there any heaps around here? I mean what do you do for work?" Paul asked a young man in well-wrinkled clothes. The man looked puzzled. "We're here because we can't get work. Have you worked lately?"

"Just a few days ago," Paul said.

"Really?" Several of the men stood up and moved over to him, forgetting whatever place they held in the line.

"Was it at the lagoon?" asked a woman.

"Naw. I betcha he means those damn spills by the power plant. I'd rather rot in hell than shovel that shit up," growled an older man.

"PCB's, man? Was you doing that?" A short man with long hair sucked a wrinkled cigarette.

"No, I was tearing bumpers off old cars," Paul said, realizing that few, if any, had come from the landfill.

"You were a mechanic? You won't get any soup if you were working," said another.

"Why? Don't you get fed if you work?" Paul said.

"You must have an education," said a tidy young man in front of him. "I graduated from the U of S three years ago, before they shut the school. Engineering. How about you?"

"Ah, no," said Paul. "I just read."

"Oh," replied the man ahead of him. "There's no shame in teaching yourself. God knows that few have enough to buy books, let alone pay for an education. Doing away with the libraries, that was the end." The man reached out for Paul's hand, and Paul extended it. "Call me Frank. What's your name?"

"Paul."

"I should be getting a train pass in the mail any day now. My brother is paying for my family to go to Montreal. He's a dentist." He smiled at Paul, slightly embarrassed. "I'm lucky, I still have my family," he said, then looked to the doors in front of the line.

"The train?" Paul hoped Frank would tell him more.

"The passenger train service is real expensive, isn't it? I talked to a young man a few weeks ago, he was riding the rods. He said he read about how they used to do it in the Great Depression. Could anything be worse than what is happening in this country right now?"

"Okay, folks. Sorry we took so long." A large black man opened the double glass doors, and Paul saw workers inside wearing white uniforms, setting up tables. "Got potato soup this morning. Just line up over there for your Full Spectrum Test and then you can come and eat." The man pointed to the table. On it sat a white jug like the one the tribe found in the heap. "Those with children to feed are over there."

"What is that test?" Paul asked Frank who was taking small cards stamped with Family out of his pocket. "Over there with the jug?"

"When were you tested last?"

"I wasn't. The needles, they . . ." Paul thought about the story Singer told him where the Book instructed the tribe to take pills. "No, I can't be tested. I won't let them put the needles in me, not for food. I'll die."

"Hey, wait! No man. It won't hurt. Really, I was afraid of needles for a while too, but if you aren't HIV or have hepatitis then don't worry about it." Four uniformed people were setting out white balls of soft hair, white tape, white bottles.

"It won't kill me?" Paul asked.

"Hell, no," Frank replied. "Don't eat and see where that gets you. If you're Blood Disease Positive, you never know. They might even get you a ride down the street to the hospice and you'll be sitting down to a meal in no time. I've seen that happen once." Frank took Paul's arm and gently pulled him into line. The old man in front of them smiled. His teeth were gone and the black rotting roots reminded Paul of Moen.

"You never know, though, mate. I think they're making us BDP to kill us off, and make us go away quicker," the old man said, snickering.

"Don't listen to him. I've been tested lots of times and I'm fine. I'll get them to do me first, then you'll see." Frank made a face to brush off the old man's joke.

"Did you say you were from the north? The population there is really low, eh? Nothing but empty buildings, crime, garbage. Damn, that TransAtlantic Clean-Up Agreement took this province from the bread basket to the garbage can of the world!" Frank said. A woman in white tied a rubber tube around his forearm and jabbed the needle into a vein.

"See, it doesn't hurt much. Go to that lady. She'll take your blood," Frank motioned with his head. Paul extended his arm for a woman whose skin was so clean it was almost white. Paul watched the sharp steel point press into his skin and he started to jerk away.

"No, you're all right man. Just be careful with him. He's not too fond of needles. Say, where is it you're from again? Saskatoon?" the young man said, trying to distract Paul.

"No, I'm from Vanhorn," said Paul, and the needle started to sting his skin.

"Yes, this is Vanhorn," said Frank, puzzled. "We're in Vanhorn right now."

"Just sit still, damn it, Paul! We just have to clean your eyes!" said Pella.

"No," he shouted. "No needles!"

9

When Paul woke up, he wondered why he was sleeping in the van. The morning had been a cold one and he stretched his knotted muscles. The van seat was split under his shoulders, his skin marked with the rough imprints of stiff vinyl.

"I am Paul," he said slowly and saw the heap through the end of the van. "Seer of the future. Radio for the past. Named after a poet." Paul swallowed hard and stood up, arching his back until he stepped to the edge of the van. "I am a garbage picker in the Landfill called Saskatchewan. That's all." His eyes were still swollen, but he could see and keep them open without pain.

In the strange dream, he had seen what the needles were used for before they were slipped into the container, but this information added nothing to his life in the tribe, nor did it help the children that died with marks in their arms.

"Paul," called Crane from outside the van. "You'se probably still sleeping, ya poor bugger."

"No, I'm awake."

"So ya are," she said when she saw him. "I's gonna clean yer eyes. I boiled the water just like Singer told me ta do. But yer doing better now, ain't ya? We thought fer sure you was taking the train home."

"And where is she?"

"Singer and Braun left. Samatron made them go, or else."

"Or else what?"

"He said he'd open the jug and poke himself so he'd die like the children."

"Stupid thing to say," Paul said. "Who would lead the tribe?"

"The women thought 'bout goin' with them, but they didn't. Singer and Braun told 'em not ta come anyway. There's work ta do here, they said."

"And the jug?" Paul asked.

"Samatron's keeping it."

Paul shook his head and stepped off the van into the dirt. "Where did my sandals go?" He sat back down, quickly lifting his feet out of the mud."

"They's gotta be by the bench seat. Singer musta taken 'em off."

He crawled to retrieve them. "This damn mud burns like hell."

"Water's warm, wash 'em off Paul." Crane set the pail down and Paul dipped his feet in it, then shook off the water and fastened his sandals.

"Yeah," Paul said. "Now what?" Paul felt weak and empty. He didn't know where to go, what to do, how to think of what he'd witnessed.

He recognized it as the past. Those people standing in line, Cherry and her cigarettes, the children in the park, the man with the store. What were these people doing? Nothing. Just watching their world go by.

"Moen's got oatmeal on," Crane said. "I better wash out the pail like Singer said to." She turned to leave. "Looks like it's not gonna be too hot today."

***

"Look what's crawled out of the garbage," Samatron said when Paul stepped to the circle of pickers around the fire. Samatron's black hair was cleaner than usual, his face the only one smiling.

"Eat," said Moen, handing Paul a bowl, her black grin welcoming him. He sat down by Pella, who didn't look at him. No one else said anything for the whole meal. Prusha's face was red, her eyes looking as if she had been crying. Dole rocked back and forth perched on a tire. The wind blew plastic across the muddy dirt.

"The women left?" Paul asked.

"Finally," Samatron said. "They caused 'nough trouble. Eatin' our food, stirrin' up the tribe. I thought things would never be the same." Samatron glared at Paul.

"And they won't," Paul answered.

***

The van bench was too short for his legs, so Paul had moved back into his tire shelter a few days before. Here, at least, Paul could stretch out. The dirt was thick on the sheetmetal floor, and plastic had blown in while he was away. He was tired from gathering scraps and bolts into a bucket that morning. The train was almost full.

A vision had not come to him since he dreamed about the needles in the jug. He didn't know if he'd ever have another radio dream, and he stopped waiting. He wondered if he could stand living if he never learned another new idea, or saw something more real than the garbage, the dying pickers, the cold nights.

He thought about Singer, her brown eyes luminous before she wrapped the cloth around her head. If it wasn't for her, he wouldn't be alive right then. Or at least he wouldn't have his sight.

"Paul, ya sleeping?" It was China. "I brought ya some tea."

"Tea?"

"Hot water and some leaves. Braun left us some of these pouches to colour the water. Makes it easier to drink."

Paul sipped from the cup. "It tastes better."

"Cleans your body out," China said. "Look, I'm glad yer okay."

"I have those women to thank."

"Yes. They helped us all."

"Crane said you and some others were going to go with them."

"We were," she said, lowering her head. "We still might if things don't get better here. Braun said we should stay though. They'll come back in a while and see if we're all right." She put her hand to her mouth. "Oh-no. I shouldn't have said that."

"What?"

"Don't tell Samatron the women are coming back. They said it would be a long time, anyway. We're trying real hard not ta make him mad."

"Why didn't you just let him contaminate himself with the needles? If he had died, you could have done whatever you wanted."

"I may not always agree with Samatron but I like him. We had a baby together once." China was kicking at a lump in the dirt and Paul noticed it was electrical gar, which the train sometimes requested. The ends of a cord had been plugged into each other, permanently joined by time, while the cord had long since been severed in the middle.

"Not just that, either," China continued, "none of us knows how to read in this tribe. What would we do with the Book from the train? Samatron agreed to ask the East for bandages, pills, more water for when the women are with babies. We coulda never wrote that down by ourselves. Braun and Singer said they had work in their own tribe, that they'd help us get started but we had ta do it ourselves."

"You women want babies now?"

"Not with the tribe like this, that's for sure."

"I thought you could read."

"Just a little. I can make out the sounds of letters. Braun said that everyone in their tribe is taught ta read."

"I can read, but I don't know if I'd make a great boss."

China looked away. "What bothers me is that jug. We can't do anything he doesn't like as long as he can threaten us with it."

"Did you really think he would?"

"Kill himself? Yeah. He was crazy like Crane on a bad day, shouting and pushing the older men. He thought we were all just going ta walk down the track and leave him. With his jumping like that, we wanted ta, but I felt for him. I guess I saw how lonely he'd be."

Paul said nothing.

"He's not a bad boss, either. He can be kind, and he's strong. He does his best and knows how ta keep the tribe working hard. But things gotta change."

"I've said that for years." Paul kicked at the plastic scraps with his feet. The space the women sometimes cleared was covered again in scraps and paper.

"Yes, but you never did anything ta show us."

Off to the side, someone stepped on a piece of plastic. Samatron's face appeared behind some stacked white washing machines.

"Hi," said Paul, and China turned to leave in the other direction.

"China," Samatron said, reaching out for her hand. She shook him off and found another path into the heap, away from the two men.

"Looks like she's done with you," Paul said.

"You supposed ta be resting?"

"I'm weak from fighting the infection. I thought I'd sleep this afternoon."

"Best get yer strength up." Samatron looked in the direction China left. "You gonna chase that brown-haired picker?"

"I don't know."

"Paul, I didn't come ta the van when you were sick." Samatron shifted his weight, studying the gar-bags, torn and wet, beside the path that China took. "I know the gar comes up in the night, even on us men who aren't old. I guess I'm always wondering in the back of my mind, what is it like ta die. You were close, Paul.

The women said it. Those two pale ones, they were even bothered, but I didn't know what ta do. I —"

"You thought if I died, then you could be next."

"Makes a guy think." Samatron cleared his throat, and shifted his weight to the other foot. "Well, if you're going ta stay in my tribe, ya better work hard." Samatron marched down the path after China.

Paul crawled back into his shelter and closed his eyes. Instantly he saw a small baby, and though he had only seen such a young child once before, Paul knew this vision-baby was newborn. The naked child moved its lips, sucking from the swollen tit, shaping itself into the cleft of its mother's arm. Blue veins, like branches from the trees he dreamed about, laced the breast.

But as Paul tried to see the top of her shoulders, the mother's face faded. Paul sighed, hoping the sucking infant would be his own.

The sun wasn't hot, but still he could feel his skin burning again. Somewhere, not far away, was a tribe of pickers with hats and clear skin.

Their children lived, their people read, their days were better than Paul's days. There was an oil-eyed woman who knew her mind, who might want to talk with him again.

He could hide in the train, wait until it pulled out, and jump off when it passed the other heap, but what would Singer say? Maybe she was right. He had to make a difference in his own tribe first.

China said that the women would return in time to check on them. Paul didn't know what Singer would think then. But he knew what he wanted her to think. It wasn't enough that his vision grew to show the Saskatchewan that had once been. Other than his complaining, Paul lived his life as if he never had the dreams at all, as if he knew just as little as everyone else. For too long Paul had grumbled that no one listened to him. Singer had only seen that side of him.

Now, Paul had to sleep. He had to rest so he would grow strong again. He would drink the tea, eat the food, and pick in the heap. But Paul knew what else he had to do — not in the same way he knew things when he had the radio dreams. This was a strong knowing that started inside his gut and made him determined. He imagined how he would fashion a new shelter for himself. Something warmer, cleaner, bigger than old vans. And when his shelter was done, he would make one for Moen, and then for each of the others. One by one, when he had time.

And when he was getting a better sleep, he would use his spare time to pick that place clean. The women would be surprised to see him moving the large metal drums, the bed springs, the broken shelves, the rusting pipes, the shredded black tires, so that the soil itself might catch an idea or a vision from somewhere, and grow green.

Then a different wind blew warmly over his face, drying his eyes, and he had no choice but to breathe in its sweetness, to be fed by its power as if the wind was no longer a pointless entity in Vanhorn, but the force of everything Paul wanted.

"I am Paul," he said. He knew his other ideas would take time to build. Maybe if Singer came back that way, she could help him. "The doer. Named after a poet."